HAPPY BIRTHDAY, MONSTER!

Scott Beck

Abrams Books for Young Readers
New York

Artist's note:
The art in this book was created with acrylic paint on illustration board.

Library of Congress Cataloging-in-Publication Data:

Beck, Scott.
Happy birthday, Monster! / by Scott Beck.
p. cm.
Summary: Ben throws a surprise birthday party for his
friend and fellow monster, Doris, complete with dancing,
snacks, games, and presents.
ISBN-13: 978-0-8109-9363-1 (hardcover)
ISBN-10: 0-8109-9363-5 (hardcover)
[1. Birthdays—Fiction. 2. Parties—Fiction. 3. Monsters—Fiction.] I. Title.
PZ7.B3809Hap 2007
[E]—dc22
2006035485

Text and illustrations copyright © 2007 Scott Beck

Book design by Chad W. Beckerman

Published in 2007 by Abrams Books for Young Readers,
an imprint of Harry N. Abrams, Inc.

Printed and bound in China
10 9 8 7 6 5 4 3 2 1

HNA ▌▌▌▌▌
harry n. abrams, inc.
a subsidiary of La Martinière Groupe
115 West 18th Street
New York, NY 10011
www.hnabooks.com

For my parents

Ben is throwing a surprise party for his friend Doris.

The guests arrive right on time.

They can't wait to yell,

"Happy birthday!"

Then the party starts.

Ben is quite a host.

The guests are having a great time,

eating snacks . . .

and listening to music.

In fact, everyone is getting along so well

that they decide to dance.

And play games.

They bounce in the parachute . . .

and jump rope . . .

and hit the piñata.

Before they know it,

it's time for cake.

Everyone gets a piece.

And when the party's over . . .

Doris says, "Thanks, Ben. You think of everything."